Pinocchio

Story retold by Janet Brown
Illustrations by Ken Morton

Gepetto the woodcarver made wonderful toys. All the children loved him. But Gepetto was lonely. More than anything, he wished for a son of his own.

So one day he made himself a wooden puppet. When he pulled the strings, the puppet danced and seemed alive. Gepetto called him Pinocchio.

What did Gepetto wish for more than anything else in the world?

At night Gepetto looked up at the night sky. "Please send me a son!" he whispered.

When he was asleep, the Blue Fairy appeared. "Wake up, Pinocchio!" she said, and the puppet came to life! His strings fell away and he danced a jig all by himself.

"If you are honest, brave and unselfish, I will make you a real boy," promised the Blue Fairy. "Until then, Jiminy Cricket will be your conscience."

What did the Blue Fairy promise Pinocchio?

Gepetto was delighted with his new son. He bought him some books and sent him to school.

On the way Pinocchio met a sly young fox and a mean old cat. "We can make you famous!" they told him. "Come and dance at Stromboli's Puppet Show – you'll be a star!"

"Don't go!" warned Jiminy Cricket. "Think of Gepetto!"

But Pinocchio wanted to be a star.

Who did Pinocchio meet on his way to school?

Pinocchio danced at Stromboli's and everybody clapped. But at night he was locked in a cage and left alone. Pinocchio knew Gepetto would be worried. He wished he had listened to Jiminy.

When the Blue Fairy appeared, Pinocchio didn't want her to know how vain he had been. So he told her: "Two monsters kidnapped me!" As he went on lying, his nose grew longer and longer.

"Lies grow, just like your nose is growing," said the Blue Fairy. "I will set you free, but you must learn from this lesson!"

Why did Pinocchio's nose start growing longer and longer?

Pinocchio started for home. But on the way he saw the sly young fox and the mean old cat. "Come with us to the fair!" they said. "All the other boys are having lots of fun!"

"Don't go!" warned Jiminy Cricket. "Think of Gepetto!"

But Pinocchio wanted to play with other boys.

Why does Pinocchio want to follow the sly young fox
and the mean old cat?

The boys played all day long. They didn't know that they would pay for their fun. They didn't know that soon they would turn into donkeys and be taken away…

"Look at your funny ears!" said Pinocchio, pointing to the other boys. He thought it was a joke. Then he put his hand to his *own* head and felt two large, furry ears coming through his cap. He had behaved like a donkey and now he was turning into one!

What kind of animal are all the little boys turning into?

Loyal Jiminy Cricket helped him to escape. They ran home to Gepetto – but the house was in darkness.

A bird told them what had happened. Gepetto had gone to sea to look for Pinocchio and an enormous whale had eaten his boat. Now he sat in the belly of a whale in the middle of the ocean.

Pinocchio was afraid of water but he knew what he must do – he must rescue Gepetto!

What happened to Gepetto while Pinocchio was away?

Pinocchio and Jiminy walked along the bottom of the ocean until they saw the whale. Inside the whale's belly Gepetto was fishing. Imagine his surprise when he found Pinocchio at the end of his line!

Pinocchio lit a fire and soon the whale gave a gigantic sneeze. Gepetto, Pinocchio and Jiminy flew out of his mouth in a cloud of smoke. Gepetto could not swim, so Pinocchio pulled him all the way to the beach.

When Pinocchio knew his father was safe, he collapsed.

How did Pinocchio make the whale sneeze?

"My son is dead," wailed Gepetto.

"No," said the Blue Fairy. "Your son is strong, brave and unselfish – and he is alive!"

It was true. Pinocchio stood up and he was a flesh-and-blood boy.

Jiminy was very proud. "You don't need me anymore," he said. "You have your own conscience now!"

Why did the Blue Fairy turn Pinocchio into a flesh-and-blood boy?

On a piece of paper practise writing these words.
Can you find them again in the story?

long nose

book

whale

donkey ears

paint brushes